PUGGLETON PARK

For Keaton, a most talented editor indeed—DK

For Mum—HP

PENGUIN WORKSHOP
An imprint of Penguin Random House LLC, New York

First published in the United States of America by Penguin Workshop,
an imprint of Penguin Random House LLC, New York, 2024

Text copyright © 2024 by Deanna Kizis
Illustrations copyright © 2024 by Penguin Random House LLC

PENGUIN is a registered trademark and PENGUIN WORKSHOP
is a trademark of Penguin Books Ltd, and the W colophon is a registered
trademark of Penguin Random House LLC.

Visit us online at penguinrandomhouse.com.

Library of Congress Cataloging-in-Publication Data is available.

Printed in the United States of America

ISBN 9780593661246 (paperback)
ISBN 9780593661253 (library binding)

2nd Printing

LSCC

Design by Jay Emmanuel

PUGGLETON PARK

by Deanna Kizis
illustrated by Hannah Peck

Penguin Workshop

Chapter One

It is a truth everyone knows that all dogs need a forever home, and for Penelope the pug, this was no different.

Penelope was a stray in Puggleton Park, you see, although it was not always this way. She had a collar, and a name tag, which meant she had an owner. But for the life of her, Penelope could not find the Lady to whom she belonged.

If you have ever been to Puggleton Park, then you know it's a *lovely* place right in the center of London. There are acres of grass to picnic upon, beds of bluebells to sniff, and a bubbling brook from which to drink. If you stand in just the right spot, you can even catch a glimpse of Buckingham Palace looking ever so much like a tall, frosted wedding cake.

Everyone in the city loved to visit Puggleton Park—especially Penelope. A kindly pup just shy of eleven months old, she was fond of gnawing bones, playing fetch, and eating dog biscuits. She was also well known for kissing humans she especially liked, and her manner was gentle, although she was rather untrained. This was not

Penelope's fault, of course, but the fault of her Lady's—a caring woman who simply could not help spoiling her dog.

On the day Penelope got lost, she and her Lady had been having a *most* splendid time. They played fetch near a grove of old oak trees, picked bluebells from the field, cooled their feet in the bubbling brook, and finally found the perfect spot for a well-deserved picnic.

While her dear Lady ate raspberry tarts, which were her favorite, Penelope lay at her feet, chewing the dog biscuit she always got as a special treat. Feeling satisfied, Penelope gazed at two nearby fox terriers who were rolling over one another in a pretend battle that was growing most energetic indeed.

"Come play with us!" one of the
terriers said during a brief pause in the
match.

"No, thank you," Penelope said, rolling over with a yawn. The sun was warming her belly, you see, and it made her drowsy. *Besides, I prefer the company of my Lady to any other,* Penelope thought, just as her owner reached over to give her a scratch and a pat. *There is no reason to move.*

Suddenly, something caught her eye.

Oh, but it was the most *dreadful* squirrel.

I should say now that Penelope did not care for squirrels in general, but this one was more dreadful than most, with his ratty tail, shifty eyes, and huge buckteeth. She watched in dismay as he darted up to her Lady's picnic basket, plucked up a raspberry tart, and ran.

But this simply would not do! So,
like any good pug defending her Lady's
property, Penelope barked, "Stop,
thief!" and raced after her prey.

And what a race it was!

Penelope chased Dreadful Squirrel past the playing puppies, through the field of bluebells, and over the bubbling brook. They raced past the old oak trees and dashed across a green meadow, zigzagging this way and that. She *almost* caught him near Swan Pond, his tail a mere acorn's length away from her snapping jaws, but at the last moment, Dreadful Squirrel darted up a tree with a taunting "Pleased to make your acquaintance!" And just like that, he—and the raspberry tart—were gone.

Oh, but Penelope was *furious*, for she truly hated to lose. However, she was also wise enough to know when it was time to accept defeat and go back the way she came.

She looked to the right and saw nothing but trees. She looked to the left and saw nothing but grass. That was when she realized she was lost. Not a little bit lost, mind you, *a lot* bit lost.

A cloud passed over the sun, and suddenly the park loomed large and threatening. Fear began to pump in Penelope's veins, and worry struck

her brain like lightning. There was a
loud clap of thunder overhead, and
she did a *most* unfortunate thing: She
started to run blindly forward in the
first direction her little legs could
take her!

She ran, and she ran, and she *ran*.
The question, of course, is whether
Penelope was running toward her Lady,
but I'm afraid she was not.

You must get a hold of yourself, Penelope! she thought as she stopped to catch her breath. After a few moments, she was calm, and put her nose to the ground to try to find a way back. But to her dismay, her trail went thisaway then thataway, then *every* which way.

As the skies darkened, Penelope's friend Moon rose high in the sky. Tired and hungry, she realized she would not find her Lady that night. *There is nothing worse than to want something so desperately*, she thought, *only to find one has not the energy to seek it.*

She spied a nearby park bench and decided it would have to serve as her shelter for the night. So she curled up, feeling lonely, vexed, terrified—and very hungry indeed!

Penelope's last thought as she drifted off to sleep was that she would surely find her Lady the next day. For anything else to happen would be too horrible! And horrible things didn't happen to pugs. They simply *didn't.* Yet in the back of her mind a thought wiggled: *But what if they do?*

CHAPTER TWO

When Penelope awoke, a heavy rain had fallen in the night, and the ground was soggy. She took a sniff of dirt and that's when she realized that any chance of finding the trail back to her Lady had been washed away.

"Well, what is it we have here?" asked a duck who was on a morning stroll with her ducklings. "A pug on her own in the park? I have never seen the like!"

"And I do not like to be
the first," said Penelope. "But,
you see, I've lost my Lady. Perhaps
you've seen her?"

"How would I know?" said the duck.
"Since I've never seen *you*?"

Penelope introduced herself and
proceeded to describe her Lady. She
was very tall (of course, to a pug, all
humans are) and had a delightful scent
that reminded Penelope of fresh red
apples.

"I'm afraid I've seen no such human," said the duck. "Although I only pay attention to the humans who throw bread in Swan Pond, and even then I barely notice them."

"It could be worse, I suppose," said Penelope.

"Why do you say that?" asked the duck.

"Because I'm certain my Lady is looking for me."

"But what if she isn't?"

"Isn't what?"

"Isn't looking for you?"

Penelope paused at this frightful thought, then quickly put it out of her mind.

"She is," she said. "She simply must be."

"I wouldn't know about such things," said the duck, as wisps of clouds floated across the sky like cotton candy. "But if you can't find *your* Lady, then I'm afraid you will become a *lone*."

"What is a lone?"

"A lone is a lost dog who has no Lady."

"But I don't want to be a lone," said Penelope.

"Who would?" said the duck. She turned and walked away, instructing her ducklings to follow, for they had lingered far too long.

For the rest of the day, Penelope searched for her Lady to no avail. Then she searched the next day, and the day after that, and even more days after *that*. But weeks passed, and Penelope could not find her Lady, nor did her Lady find her.

Sometimes Penelope would see ladies and gentlemen walking their dogs, and she'd call out, "Have you seen my Lady?" But neither hound nor poodle had seen her anywhere.

Penelope realized she simply had to accept the truth: She *was* a lone.

CHAPTER THREE

If you feel terribly sad about Penelope being lost in Puggleton Park, do not despair.

She had gotten herself into the worst sort of trouble, it's true, but she was also resilient.

If you don't know what *resilient* means, let me tell you now: A pug—or a human, or a toad, or any other kind of creature—who is resilient is able to handle all kinds of difficulty, whether it's a meal made of mushy vegetables, stepping on a red ant nest, or being very lost indeed.

Because she was resilient, Penelope soon figured out how to make her way in Puggleton Park.

In the morning, she ate the delicious scraps that people dropped from their picnic baskets. At midday, she took herself for a walk along the brook and organized her thoughts.

In the afternoon, she chased Dreadful Squirrel—who was quite dreadful, after all—but he always got away somehow or other.

In the evenings, she either frolicked in the rose gardens outside the Grand Hall, or if there was a ball, Penelope was sure to attend.

She did not go inside, of course. Even a pug needs an invitation for *that*.

Yet Penelope believed that happiness could be found outside a ball just as easily as it could be found inside. So she sat near the entrance and watched the ladies of London come and go.

Their colorful clothes and hairstyles were very grand indeed, but Penelope wasn't there just to watch. Each time a lady got out of her carriage, she sniffed

the air, hoping to recognize her Lady's
familiar scent. But, to her dismay, she
never did.

One night, after another ball,
Penelope curled up under her favorite
bench and snuggled into a pale green

velvet coat that someone had lost in the park, which she now cleverly used as a bed. (That's how resilient she was.)

Why do people lose so many things in the park? Penelope wondered as she stared at her friend Moon. *People have a great many things, but they cannot keep track of most of them. Not even pugs.*

But what could she do? She was, after all, much too small to do anything big in this world.

Moon's belly was as full as a puppy's at Christmas. Sometimes she was large. Other times she was just a tiny sliver. Sometimes Moon was not there at all. Yet all the animals knew the power of Moon, whether she was crescent or full, present or missing. The birds flew where Moon sent them. The raccoons found food in her light. Time was told by her comings and goings. Even oceans moved by the way of Moon.

"One cannot simply lie there doing nothing, Penelope," Moon said, big and bright in the night sky. "Large or small, we all have a part to play in the world."

Penelope had to admit that Moon had a point. So, by her silver light, she made a very important decision: If her Lady could not find her, she would simply have to go out and find her Lady herself.

Chapter Four

The very next night, Penelope was sitting outside another ball when she noticed a lady shivering in a pale green velvet dress. Then she realized why—she was without a coat!

Not having a coat is a very unfortunate thing, Penelope thought. *After all, I am most unwilling to go anywhere without mine.*

Wait! she thought. *I have an idea!*

She raced across Puggleton Park, found her park bench, and grabbed the cozy green coat she used as a bed. Then she ran as fast as she could with the coat in her mouth, tugging it over branches, leaves, and mud.

I hope that lady is still there! Penelope thought.

And she was.

Penelope was very proud as she walked up to the lady and laid the pale green velvet coat at her feet.

"Oh, my goodness!" the lady cried. "I do believe that is my coat!"

Indeed, it *was* her coat. The same coat that Lady Diggleton, as she was known, had lost in the park earlier in the year.

She reached for the coat, and Lady

Picklebottom, who considered it her duty to tell her closest friend what to do at all times, became most alarmed.

"Don't touch that, Lady Diggleton!" she said. "That coat is filthy! Just look at the rips! Look at the mud! I daresay this pug found your coat and used it as some sort of bed!"

Lady Diggleton thought a moment, and said, "If that's the case, then she must be a very clever pug indeed."

The kind lady leaned down and reached for the little pug's collar. "So your name is Penelope," she said.

Penelope wagged her tail.

"My name is Lady Diggleton. I do believe you must be lost."

Penelope wagged her tail again.

"I shall have my footman summon

the dogcatcher at once," said Lady Picklebottom, raising a finger.

"There's no need," said Lady Diggleton. "I'm taking this pug home with me."

Lady Picklebottom's eyes widened. "I must tell you, my dearest friend, that this is far from wise," she said.

"Animals are noisy—and dirty, too. Which is why it has long been my firm belief that animals belong on a farm."

She leaned in and laid a hand on Lady Diggleton's arm. "And do not forget that you have been through so much this year. You need peace and quiet."

Lady Diggleton nodded. "I appreciate your kind advice, Lady Picklebottom," she said. "But I simply cannot leave this pug out here in the cold. She can spend the night with me, and in the morning, I will begin to search for her owner."

The next thing Penelope knew, Lady Diggleton got into her carriage and a footman placed her in the lady's lap. Then Lady Diggleton tucked her under the pale green velvet coat, and

Penelope felt ever so warm. *Tomorrow she will help me find my Lady!* Penelope thought as sleep began to make her eyes heavy. *And then I will be able to go home at last.*

CHAPTER FIVE

The next morning, Penelope opened her eyes and realized that she was lying on a green velvet pillow that perfectly matched a nearby green canopy bed. All around her was floral wallpaper festooned with flowers and birds. Clearly, she was in someone's bedroom. But whose bedroom was it? And whose house?

Oh yes! she remembered. *There was a ball. There was a coat. There was a lady whose last name was Diggleton . . .*

Penelope sat up with a start. Lady Diggleton was going to help her find her Lady, and her days as a lone would be over at last!

Without warning, a young woman with a dutiful face, wearing a simple but clean brown dress, walked in.

"I'm Abby, the lady's maid," she said, "and you must be the pug I've been hearing about all morning." She started to make Lady Diggleton's bed. "I, for one, can't believe it. A pug? In this house? As if I don't have enough to do?"

Penelope gazed at the lady's maid, tilting her head in thought. Abby really didn't need to do anything on her account, except bring her to Lady Diggleton.

"I've got the sewing, mind you, and the shopping, too," Abby continued. "But I've been told to get you ready. Get a pug ready! I've never heard of such a thing! Doesn't everyone know *I have so much to do*?"

Abby picked Penelope up like a sack of potatoes and brought her into the largest bathroom she had ever seen, inside of which was the *most* gigantic tub she had ever seen, inside of which was the most *enormous* mountain of bubbles she had ever seen. But before Penelope could so much as whimper, Abby plunged her into the suds and began to give her the most ferocious bath she'd ever received.

It was as though Abby had six hands:
two to keep Penelope's scrambling body
in the water, two to scrub her back and
belly, and two to splash suds all
over her ears and face.

"You must stop wriggling,
Penelope!" Abby cried.

"You'll only make this take longer, and I've got ever so much to do!"

When Abby was finished, she plucked the pug from the tub and wrapped her up in a towel like a sausage in a bun. Then she attacked Penelope's nails with trimmers until they were properly clipped and brushed her coat with brisk strokes until it shone. And while Penelope did enjoy a brush behind the ears now and then, having *all* her fur brushed was not her favorite experience, to say the least. But all was forgiven when Abby held up a looking glass.

The little pug gazed at her reflection and could not deny that she liked what she saw.

"So," Abby said to the pug, "was it really as bad as all that?"

Penelope looked at her, unsure. Being clean was not an unpleasant sensation, but if that was how Abby gave a dog a bath, it was something she would happily skip for the rest of her days!

Penelope followed the maid's quickly moving heels through the house.

"That's the dressing room," Abby said as they passed a room filled with Lady Diggleton's dresses. "I have to clean that."

"That's the kitchen," she said as they

passed a large oven that gave off warm smells, making Penelope's tummy growl. "I don't have to clean that."

"And this," she said as she opened a door, "is the garden, where dogs do their business."

Oh, but Penelope was ever so relieved to be let out. She really did have a lot of business to do!

"I'll definitely have to clean *that*," Abby said with a grumble when Penelope was done. "As if I don't have enough to do."

Back inside, Penelope followed Abby down a long hall, where her eyes were drawn to a painted portrait of a kind-looking gentleman in a pale green velvet coat. Noticing her stare, Abby stopped a moment.

"That is Lord Diggleton," she said. "When he died in that horrible carriage accident last year, I thought my lady would perish of a broken heart."

Penelope stared at the portrait and felt something familiar—the feeling of losing someone you love. *And yet,* she thought, *there are some things that cannot be changed, no matter how deeply the heart wants otherwise.* Even though she was just a pug, she did understand such things, you see.

"Well," Abby said, smoothing down her dress, "enough of this dawdling about. Lady Diggleton is waiting."

At the sound of Lady Diggleton's name, Penelope remembered her kindness the night before, and how cozy it was to fall asleep in her lap.

But she was nervous, too. *Will Lady Diggleton really help me find my Lady?* she wondered. *And what will become of me if she won't?*

Chapter Six

Lady Diggleton liked to have her breakfast at a long table in a dining room with high windows and a sparkling chandelier that reminded Penelope of the stars.

"Good morning, Penelope," she said to the pug when she appeared in the doorway. "Come in! Your breakfast is waiting."

Breakfast? For me? This was enough to

get Penelope to run across the room and jump right into Lady Diggleton's lap!

"Bad dog! No!" sputtered Abby.

"Well," Lady Diggleton said, looking at Penelope and laughing, "this is a surprise. But I find I'm not opposed."

Breakfast consisted of a little silver bowl that was filled to the brim with kitchen scraps of the finest quality—bits of crisp potatoes, fresh peas, and salted ham—while her water was clear and cool. Penelope ate and drank until her tummy was quite full, then she burped a little pug burp.

"My, you were hungry," Lady Diggleton said, reaching for a crystal jar. She took out not one but two freshly baked dog biscuits, which she'd asked the cook, Miss Bakerbeans, to prepare that morning. She gently held out her hand and offered them to Penelope. Ever so happy, the pug gobbled them up and licked her lips to catch every crumb, then gave Lady Diggleton a kiss right on the tip of her nose!

"Now, *that's* going a bit too far," said Abby.

"You know, I found I rather enjoyed it!" said Lady Diggleton.

"Have it your way," Abby said, turning to go. "I have so much work to do."

"And we have a mystery to solve, isn't that so, Penelope?" Lady Diggleton said. "You have a collar, which means that you have an owner. And since your collar is well made,

I do believe your owner must have the means to live somewhere quite near. So here's what we shall do: We'll knock on every door in Mayfair until we find your home!"

Hearing this, Penelope's hopes soared. Being reunited with her Lady would be wonderful indeed! But then her thoughts took a darker turn: What if her Lady didn't want her anymore? For Penelope could not get the thought out of her mind—how did she know her Lady was looking for her?

"Don't worry, Penelope," Lady Diggleton said, scratching the pug behind her left ear. (Which happened to be her favorite spot and sent her right leg kicking, fur flying everywhere in a way that would have made Abby most displeased.) "I have a feeling this will not be so very difficult. We shall find your Lady today if it's the last thing we do!"

CHAPTER SEVEN

Lady Diggleton did not own a leash, so she cleverly attached a short leather horse lead to Penelope's collar. "Are you ready?" she said.

Penelope wagged her tail.

"Then let's go!"

Lady Diggleton and Penelope stepped out into the bright noonday sun. The pug didn't know precisely where they were, but I can tell you

that they were in the most fashionable
neighborhood in London. There
were many well-dressed people
on Grosvenor Street that day, but
Penelope could hardly see more
than the bottoms of skirts, trousers,
slippers, and boots. She didn't mind,
for the air was filled with the most
delightful smells—those of horses,

people, cobblestones, and brick.
Eventually, she caught a glimpse of
the surrounding homes, which were
painted in bright white with tall
windows and imposing doors. The
houses marched up the street in an
orderly fashion, and many of them
looked curiously the same. But for the
life of her, Penelope could not recall if

she'd ever lived in a home so grand.

Isn't it strange that a dog would not be able to remember what her own home looks like? This is because dogs do not find where they live by sight, but by smell. So as Lady Diggleton walked up the street, her head held high and her chestnut hair glinting in the sun, Penelope put her nose to the ground, sniffing for anything that smelled familiar, yet nothing did.

At the first door, Lady Diggleton knocked, and Penelope sat at her feet, nervous and excited. A footman wearing a blue coat with shiny buttons answered.

"Hello," Lady Diggleton said. "Could you tell me if you've ever seen this pug?"

The footman considered the pug and shook his head. "Sadly not, my lady," he said.

"Quite all right!" said Lady Diggleton brightly as the door snapped shut. She looked down at Penelope. "Don't despair. One could hardly expect the first house to be the one. On we go."

They walked to the next house, and once again Lady Diggleton knocked on the door. Penelope tried to keep calm as a footman wearing a black coat with shiny buttons answered. "Hello," Lady Diggleton said. "Could you tell me if you've ever seen this pug?"

He looked down at Penelope and frowned. "I must say I have not, my lady."

They walked down the steps, and

Lady Diggleton said, "Of course, expecting the second house to be the one would be far too easy."

But then she knocked on the next door, and the one after that, and too many to count after that, and the answer was always the same.

"Sorry, my lady."

"No, my lady."

"I'm afraid not, my lady."

Penelope's paws began to ache, and Lady Diggleton's brightness began to fade. She sat down on a park bench in Grosvenor Square, and Penelope lay miserably at her feet.

"I'm sorry, Penelope," said Lady Diggleton. "I truly believed we would find your home today. But I was wrong."

Penelope peered up at Lady Diggleton, eyes filled with sadness. She'd long feared she would never find her Lady, but that fear seemed to be hardening into fact.

Sensing her despair, Lady Diggleton picked up the little pug and placed her in her lap.

"I have also felt grief and loss," she said. "And it stung all the more because I could not say a final goodbye to my dear husband. One moment he was getting in a carriage, and then he was gone. I felt ever so much sorrow. But life goes on in the most difficult of times, just as it does in the most wonderful."

Penelope sighed. She appreciated Lady Diggleton's words, but that didn't mean she wanted to spend the rest of her days without a Lady to call her own. For a pug without a Lady was like a sock without a foot, or a bone without a dog. Whatever would she do?

Chapter Eight

The sun rose bright and happy, but
Penelope stayed in bed. Her tummy
was empty, yet she had no desire to
eat. Her mouth was dry, yet she had no
desire to drink. Her spirits were low
indeed, and if you have ever been so
unhappy, then you know that staying
in bed is the only sensible thing to do.
Every now and again, Abby would peer
in and eye the floor where Penelope

had been shedding—she'd have to clean that, of course—but she said nothing.

It was after eleven when Lady Diggleton entered the room and said, "There you are, Penelope! It's time to get up, for we are going to tea!"

Tea? thought Penelope, her ears perking up. *As in a tea "party"?*

She'd seen children playing tea party in the park, so of course she understood exactly what this was. Tea parties involved playing, chasing one another around, a fine meal of tasty sandwiches and biscuits, and frolicking. Oh, Penelope had always wanted to go to tea! And now she finally would.

Penelope's tail did not stop wagging the entire way up Brook Street. As she and Lady Diggleton climbed the steps of another grand house, she could barely contain her excitement. A footman in a yellow coat with a powdered wig opened the door. He then led them to a yellow sitting room where Penelope recognized the one person in the world she would rather not see, and who would rather not see her. "My dear Lady Diggleton!" Lady Picklebottom exclaimed. "I see you've brought that stray dog with you!"

"I have indeed," said Lady Diggleton, entering a drawing room with walls covered in yellow fabric so bright that it stung the eye. "While I know how you feel about dogs, I do believe you will enjoy Penelope's company as much as I do."

"Well, I know so little about animals, of course," Lady Picklebottom said, motioning for Lady Diggleton to sit in a bright yellow chair. "But a dog, in my most humble opinion, does do best on a farm."

She leaned down to Penelope, saying loudly, "Wouldn't you adore that? To live on a farm?"

It was all Penelope could do not to growl as she jumped into Lady Diggleton's lap.

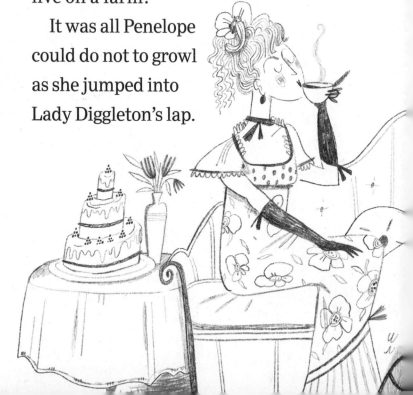

At this, Lady Picklebottom raised an eyebrow—allowing a dog to sit on one's lap was, in her eyes, very disturbing indeed. But more guests were arriving, and so she decided to say nothing of it.

Soon several ladies were seated around the room, and Penelope prepared herself to be showered with biscuits and affection.

However, to her surprise and dismay, the women ignored her completely! They simply talked, and talked, and *talked*. They chittered the way birds sang in the trees. They chattered the way chipmunks did in the bushes. They did not stop chittering or chattering as one moment stretched into the next.

Penelope was confused. Wasn't a tea party supposed to be fun? And as for whether the biscuits on the table were as delicious as they smelled, well, Penelope didn't know, as none were offered to her. Penelope grew weary just sitting there. But when Lady Diggleton gave her a small pat on the head and said, "You're being a very good pug, Penelope," she allowed herself a satisfied sigh. If Lady Diggleton was happy, then Penelope was prepared to endure the dullest tea party in all the world.

She was just falling asleep when she noticed it: a flash of red fur, just beyond the window, and the sound of rustling leaves. Then Penelope saw the flicker of a suspicious black eye, followed by a ragged tail, and buckteeth.

It was Dreadful Squirrel!

But before Penelope could so much as bark, he dashed through Lady Picklebottom's open window and

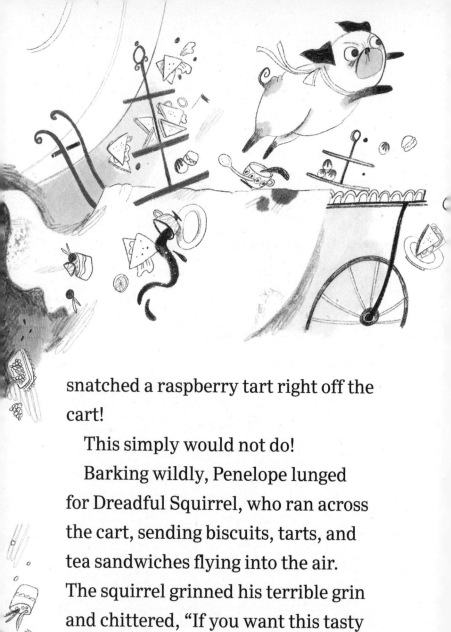

snatched a raspberry tart right off the cart!

This simply would not do!

Barking wildly, Penelope lunged for Dreadful Squirrel, who ran across the cart, sending biscuits, tarts, and tea sandwiches flying into the air. The squirrel grinned his terrible grin and chittered, "If you want this tasty

morsel back, you'll have to come and
get it!"

"Challenge accepted!" Penelope
barked in return, racing after him as
he leaped from the dessert cart to the
lavender sofa to the drapes. Over the
tea table they went, under the desk,
behind a screen, and through the
ashes in the fireplace.

Lady Picklebottom's drawing
room was soon destroyed, and then
Penelope chased Dreadful Squirrel
right

out

the

open

window.

The ladies rushed to see what would
happen next. Oh, but it was not a pretty
sight! Penelope, in her haste, had flung
herself out the window and soared
after Dreadful Squirrel as though she
could fly. It turned out, however, that
she could not.

This is how the ladies found Penelope
in the bushes below, with her bottom
in the air, and the rest of her stuck in
a hedgerow. Struggling to free herself,

Penelope wriggled and wiggled until she was able to pop her head out of the bush with a leaf stuck on her nose. As she looked at it cross-eyed, Lady Diggleton could not hold it in any longer—she started to laugh and laugh.

But the other ladies were *not* amused.

"Goodness me, what's wrong with that pug?" exclaimed Lady Barton.

"And what's wrong with that squirrel?" said Lady Pemberley.

"You must find the dog's owner at once," insisted Lady Donwell.

"Just send her away to a farm!" yelled Lady Picklebottom. "And you, my dear friend," she said, turning to Lady Diggleton. "What is it that you find so funny? Is it my shattered teapot? My destroyed drawing room? I don't understand your behavior at all!"

Lady Diggleton apologized most sincerely for all the damage done, promising to pay for everything. Then she checked Penelope for thorns, of which, thankfully, there were none. As they walked home, Penelope tried not to whimper. She had ruined the tea party, something Lady Picklebottom would not soon forgive, and embarrassed Lady Diggleton, too. Surely she would be sent away now, whether Lady Diggleton found her original Lady or not.

And the worst part of all was that she'd become rather fond of Lady Diggleton. Rather fond indeed.

CHAPTER NINE

Oh, poor Penelope! If there ever was a pug in a more disappointing situation, one cannot imagine it.

In the morning, she met Lady Diggleton for breakfast, but this time she could not bear to jump into her lap and felt certain Lady Diggleton wouldn't want her to.

A footman entered to announce that they had a visitor, and when Penelope

smelled Lady Picklebottom, she scooted further under Lady Diggleton's chair.

"My poor, dear friend!" Lady Picklebottom said as she entered the room. "I am so sorry for my outburst yesterday. A case of nerves, you see, brought on by ever so much excitement. Despite what I said, I must assure you, Lady Diggleton, that a ruined tea means little to me. My grandmother's china was smashed to bits, of course, but that hardly matters. What *matters* is that our friendship remains intact, as it has since our families introduced us at the tender age of four!"

Lady Diggleton opened her mouth to speak, but Lady Picklebottom continued.

"As your friend, I must say I have

become more than a little worried, for you do not seem like yourself lately. It's almost as though you prefer the dog's company to mine, but that's impossible!" Lady Picklebottom laughed. "And so, I have decided to take on this pug business myself. Before you protest, Lady Diggleton, do know that I shall not change my mind! Your very place in society is at stake!"

Lady Picklebottom put a stack of papers on the table.

"What's all that?" asked Lady Diggleton, alarmed.

"Shall I read it to you?"

Lady Diggleton nodded as Lady Picklebottom cleared her throat more loudly than one would consider polite, not that Penelope was in any position to judge such things now.

"LOST PUG!" Lady Picklebottom began to shout. "A LOST PUG WHO GOES BY THE NAME OF 'PENELOPE' HAS BEEN FOUND IN PUGGLETON PARK! IF SHE BELONGS TO YOU, *PLEASE* CONTACT LADY PICKLEBOTTOM AT 501 SOUR PATCH LANE AT ONCE!"

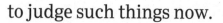

"I plan to have my footman place these flyers all over London," Lady Picklebottom said. "Pall Mall, both Oxford and Bond Streets, not to mention Puggleton Park itself. Surely someone will know the dog, and then you can return to a life of peace and quiet—and I will have the friend I know returned to me, for you can't get rid of me so easily! Now, you may think this is not what you want, but you must trust me in times like these, for only I know what you truly need."

"But—" said Lady Diggleton.

"My mind will not be changed, dear friend!" said Lady Picklebottom, getting excited again. "YOU REALLY MUST HAVE SOME PEACE AND QUIET!"

The pug's tail drooped as Lady Diggleton sighed.

Lady Picklebottom was so very overbearing, she didn't know how Lady Diggleton withstood it. *Perhaps people have different kinds of friends,* Penelope thought. *The kind you wish to keep, and the kind that stick to you like fleas.*

"Now, I must be going," Lady Picklebottom said. "The sooner this dog is reunited with her former owner, the better."

With that, Lady Picklebottom stomped from the room, bid a loud "GOOD DAY!" to the footman, and everything was quiet once more.

That night, Penelope tossed and turned, for she could find no comfort.

If only I had not chased Dreadful Squirrel, she thought. *Then I never would have lost my Lady. And if I hadn't chased him again and ruined that tea party, perhaps I could have stayed with Lady Diggleton forever. Wait.* She paused. *Did I just say that I want to stay with Lady Diggleton forever?*

This was most astonishing news, for although she loved her former Lady, she had to admit that her fondness for Lady Diggleton had grown and grown, and now she felt quite guilty.

For advice, Penelope looked up at Moon, who was a mere sliver in the night sky. "Why must my life change so, when I was content with the way it was?" she asked.

"Do you not believe that it's natural for things to change, Penelope?" Moon said. "After all, I change all the time."

"But I didn't want things to change," said Penelope.

"That may be so," said Moon. "But to deny change is to deny life and the many surprises—some difficult, some extraordinary—that come with it."

Penelope could not deny that a change had, in fact, occurred. Somehow along the way, she had let her former Lady go and had taken Lady Diggleton into her heart.

The question now, she thought, *is whether Lady Diggleton feels the same way about me.*

Unbeknownst to Penelope, Lady Diggleton was also tossing and turning, for she, too, had thoughts racing through her mind. *I find myself attached*

to that darling pug, she thought. *After all, ruining Lady Picklebottom's tea wasn't really her fault—that squirrel was absolutely dreadful! Perhaps I would enjoy having a dog of my own? It would mean having someone to love, after all.*

But then another thought came into her mind: Her husband was taken from her too soon, and the wound was still fresh. She didn't know if she could risk loving again.

Fearing she would never sleep, Lady Diggleton got up from her bed and lit a candle. She checked on Penelope, who appeared to be asleep. (In truth she was not, struggling as she was with feelings of her own.)

Lady Diggleton left the room and padded her way down the hall. She soon found herself standing before the portrait of the kind-faced man in the pale green coat.

"What should I do, my darling?" she asked the picture. She waited, but no answer came.

"What must you think of me?" she said, laughing quietly to herself. "Standing in an empty hall, asking a painting for advice . . . And yet," she said, "I do believe you can hear me sometimes, my dear.

If you can, I hope you will tell me what to do, for I am in a terrible state of confusion and cannot see which path to take."

After a few moments, Lady Diggleton turned and walked back up the hall. She climbed into her bed, and this time she did not toss and turn at all, but fell into a deep sleep.

CHAPTER TEN

In the morning, Penelope found Lady Diggleton in the sitting room, looking happier than she had the night before, the pink back in her cheeks.

"There you are, Penelope!" Lady Diggleton said, smiling. "Did you sleep well? I must say that at first, I did not. But then I fell into a deep sleep, and I had the most wonderful dream! Do you believe that you can get ideas in

dreams?" she wondered aloud to the little pug. "Well, I do believe it. I truly do. And this is one of my best ideas—although I must say I am not entirely certain it's my own."

Penelope watched, curious, as Lady Diggleton rang a little gold bell and her footman appeared. "Please tell Mr. Weeby we are ready to receive him."

The footman turned and, to Penelope's surprise, a small man with large, bushy sideburns entered the room with the air of someone who thought he was the most important person in it.

"Lady Diggleton," he said, bowing. "I am Mr. Weeby, dog trainer and master of canine etiquette. Tell me, how can I be of service?"

"It's a pleasure to meet you, Mr. Weeby," Lady Diggleton said, motioning to Penelope. "I have taken it upon myself to house this pug until I can find her rightful owner. And while

I find her to be the *most* delightful company, I do believe she would benefit by learning the ways of polite society."

"You want to train a dog you will not keep yourself?" Mr. Weeby asked.

"I would love to keep Penelope, but I still believe she belongs to another," Lady Diggleton said. "So until that mystery is solved . . ."

"She needs some manners," finished Mr. Weeby, eyeing Penelope suspiciously. "You are most generous not to turn this dog out on the street."

"I could never!" Lady Diggleton exclaimed. "This pug deserves a happy life, as do we all."

At this, Penelope could not help but wag her tail, for she agreed with the sentiment most heartily.

"Tell me, Mr. Weeby, is it true that you have trained dogs for the Queen?"

"My dear lady, my excellent manners prevent me from bragging in even the smallest way," Mr. Weeby said. "But I can say that the Queen has been known to call me the best trainer in all of England. Not that I could ever say such things about myself, of course."

"Of course," said Lady Diggleton.

"Allow me to begin my inspection of the creature," said Mr. Weeby.

To Penelope's surprise, he got down on all fours and, without the slightest introduction, stuck his face inches from hers so he could peer most rudely into her eyes as though the secrets of the universe could be found there.

Next, he donned a pair of white
gloves, and—without asking,

mind you—pried open her mouth to inspect her teeth. Of course, *that* was an affront a pug would not soon forget, and then he blew air into each of her ears. Finally, he pulled the curl of her tail out and let it bounce back again without permission, much less an apology!

"Well?" asked Lady Diggleton.

"This," Mr. Weeby announced with great seriousness, "is a pug I can train."

"Oh, thank goodness," Lady Diggleton said with a smile. "Did you hear, Penelope? Mr. Weeby is your new trainer!"

Although she did not think much of his manners, Penelope was very excited by the idea. *If I can learn to behave,* she thought, *Lady Diggleton will see that I am the most polite and well-mannered pug in all of London, and then she will never let me go.*

Mr. Weeby was her best—and only—chance.

CHAPTER ELEVEN

"Penelope shall be taught the Weeby Way," Mr. Weeby told Lady Diggleton. "It's a way that I myself invented, after much trial and error, although the truth is, I knew with *one hundred percent certainty* that it would work from the moment I thought of it. Other trainers have their methods," he added, "and I will not say anything against them. However, I have been

told many times that
the Weeby Way is,
in fact, the *only* way
to teach a dog how to
behave. Not that I would
ever say so myself, of
course."

"Of course," Lady Diggleton said, nodding. She turned to Penelope. "Now, be a good pug and listen to Mr. Weeby. As he's mentioned *many* times, you'll be in very good hands indeed."

Penelope wagged her tail as Lady Diggleton left the room, and thus began the most difficult week of her young life.

"The first thing you must learn is the Weeby Way to Sit and Stay," Mr. Weeby announced. "Dogs cannot run around saying hello to anyone and everyone. Nor can they jump on the laps of old friends or new, or cover human beings with slobbery kisses. If a person chooses to greet you—and only *if the person chooses*—you may offer your paw for a single shake.

That," he said with great seriousness, "is the only charming way a dog may greet a human being. Now, sit!" Mr. Weeby commanded, "And stay!"

Penelope did as she was asked.

"Not like that!" Mr. Weeby said. "Do not look at me. Not even for a moment. Until I indicate that you do, in fact, exist, and that you are, in fact, of interest to me, you will simply sit and do nothing," he said.

So Penelope tried to keep looking into the distance as Mr. Weeby made a great show of walking around the room pretending not to know she was there, all while she pretended not to know that he knew.

At long last, Mr. Weeby looked at Penelope as though he was surprised to see a dog in the room. "Ah, here seems to be a pug worthy of my acquaintance!" he said.

He leaned down and offered his hand. Penelope went to give Mr. Weeby a kiss. It was pure habit, of course, not a true sign of her affection for him. But before she could lick, he snatched his hand away and gave her a stern look.

"No kisses!" he said. "Do try harder. And remember, if you cannot master the Weeby Way of Sit and Stay, it shall reflect poorly upon me. Most poorly indeed!"

It took several rounds before Penelope was able to "keep her foul tongue to herself," as he called it, and, instead, offer him a single paw to shake.

Then, after a dozen more times,
which Penelope found wholly
unnecessary, Mr. Weeby seemed
satisfied.

The next day, her lesson involved
what Mr. Weeby called "the Weeby

Way: Politeness While in Motion."

"When walking in town, a well-mannered pug does not sniff about as though looking for lost lamb chops," he said as he put Penelope on a leash and led her out Lady Diggleton's front door. "And if said pug finds so much as a crumb, she most certainly doesn't eat it."

Despite Mr. Weeby, Penelope was happy to be on a walk. So happy, in fact, that she found her tail wagging. Her trainer, however, took no notice of the glorious blue sky, the heavenly smell of the flowers, or the brightness of the green grass. Instead, he continued instructing her as though they'd never left the house.

"A dog must remember their place

in society and leave people alone," he reminded her every time she turned to look up at a friendly face. "And do not forget to hold your business until you are given permission to relieve yourself in the correct place."

Mr. Weeby walked Penelope through what seemed like all of London. It was exhausting! But her speed, he said, had to match his exactly; she could be neither too fast nor too slow. She was never to tug at the leash, not to investigate another dog or, heaven forbid, another dog's behind, which, she felt most strongly, was absolutely ridiculous!

A walk through the fish market was especially difficult, as there were so many wonderful smells Penelope had to ignore. Her discontent grew as she found herself having business to do. Hours seemed to tick by as they passed bush after bush and Mr. Weeby stopped before none of them.

The poor pug was full to bursting when Mr. Weeby finally announced that he had found a small patch of grass upon which she could relieve herself. Why that patch of grass and not the hundreds of patches they had passed already, Penelope could not say, but at least she was able to enjoy the most satisfying pee the little pug could remember.

Occasionally they would come across someone Mr. Weeby knew, and he would talk about Penelope as though she did not know the sound of her own name.

"I'm working with a lost pug," he said to a lady with an Afghan hound who, Penelope had to admit, did an excellent job of employing the Weeby Way of Sit and Stay and ignored her completely. "Of course, Penelope would be difficult for any trainer, even one as talented as myself. And while I have to say I was not sure the Weeby Way would work when we began, at the same time, I was one hundred percent certain it would . . ."

One evening, they dined with Lady Diggleton, and Penelope showed her how well she could sit and stay. Meanwhile, instead of jumping into her lap and kissing her nose, she offered a single paw to shake.

"Very impressive, Mr. Weeby," said Lady Diggleton, taking Penelope's paw. "I trust the lessons are going well?"

He allowed that they were going as well as could be expected, but they had more work to do.

As Mr. Weeby ate his supper, Penelope could not help but notice that he had the most ghastly table manners! While he and Lady Diggleton talked, food seemed to drop from his fork onto the floor like rain on spring grass. First he dropped a juicy bit of roast turkey, then a plop of mouthwatering mashed potato, then a warm honey-glazed carrot.

"Is the food not to your liking, Mr. Weeby?" Lady Diggleton asked, pretending not to be the slightest bit disturbed by all the food at his feet.

"The dinner is delicious, Lady Diggleton," he replied, dropping another piece of turkey as Penelope tried not to drool. "As you can see, I am teaching Penelope not to beg, nor to 'clean' the floor. Neither is allowed in polite society, of course. And as you can see, she is passing the test—*thus far*."

"What an interesting idea," said Lady Diggleton as Mr. Weeby brushed a rainfall of bread crumbs onto the carpet. *Although,* she wondered to herself, *since when is dropping food all over my green rug considered polite?*

Penelope, meanwhile, was thinking something rather similar. *According to Mr. Weeby, it does not do for pugs to clean the floor of perfectly good food.* She stared at a tempting crust of bread that landed at her feet. *And yet I suspect he will not clean up his mess himself, either, as if Abby doesn't have enough work to do!*

As another carrot landed on the floor with a sticky thud, Penelope and Lady Diggleton both stared at it in shock. They could not speak to one another directly, of course, but they did have an understanding, for they were thinking the exact same thing: *Mr. Weeby is an absolute slob!*

CHAPTER TWELVE

The following day at tea, Mr. Weeby came running in, waving an invitation and forgetting his manners once again.

"Lady Diggleton! Lady Diggleton!" he cried.

"What is it, Mr. Weeby?" said Lady Diggleton, resisting the urge to slip Penelope a bit of biscuit under the table, for fear it would ruin her training. "You look rather excited."

"I am indeed!" he said, practically doing a dance. "For I have gotten an invitation for us to attend none other than the Begood Ball—the only ball that allows dogs! And it's the height of the season!"

Lady Diggleton nodded. "I am invited to that ball every year, as I have been friends with the Begoods for some time."

"You're most welcome," he said, ignoring what the lady had just said. "Most, most welcome. But do not feel the need to thank *me*, dear lady. No, do not thank me at all! I consider getting my clients invited to the most exclusive balls a part of my job, and I do it quite well—or so I'm told."

He sat down uninvited and helped himself to several biscuits. "I must confess I have my own reasons to attend," he said. "The Begoods' ball will give me a chance to show off Penelope's training. Who shall not be astounded by what I've done with this ill-mannered stray? Meanwhile, I am told, there is a chance that none other than the Queen will be there this year."

"Is that so?" Lady Diggleton said, suddenly paying attention, for everyone paid attention to the Queen.

"I have it on the highest authority," Mr. Weeby said. "Should this pug be called to meet the Queen, then many will take notice, and mark my words, her rightful owner shall be found!"

A ball! Penelope thought. *Actually attending a ball instead of just standing outside of one!* Oh, how Penelope longed to hear the music, to see the dancing. And while she did not believe her owner would be found, she did believe that if she was introduced to the Queen, and *if* she was able to perform the Weeby Way of Sit and Stay, surely Lady Diggleton would decide to keep her as her very own!

On the night of the ball, Abby drew Penelope yet another enormous bath. And this time she vowed not to put up a fight.

Once she was as clean as a spring rain, Abby brought Penelope into the dressing room. Penelope's eyes widened as Abby opened a velvet box and took out a small, sparkling crown, which she then ever so carefully placed upon her head. Next she tied a jade-green velvet bow around the little pug's neck. "Would you like to see yourself?" Abby asked. Penelope thought that she most certainly would indeed.

Penelope held her breath as Abby carried over a looking glass and held it up for her to see. She was astounded. *I've never been vain,* Penelope thought, *and I promise that I shall never be again. But just for tonight, I think I shall tell myself that I look most beautiful indeed.*

Also caught up in the moment, Abby attached a velvet lead to Penelope's ribbon and quietly led her downstairs to Lady Diggleton, who looked magnificent in a bright green dress.

"May I say," Abby said, in admiration, "that you two look rather perfect together?" Lady Diggleton smiled and Penelope wagged her tail. For the truth was, they did.

CHAPTER THIRTEEN

The Begoods' estate was tremendously large, and the ballroom decorations so spectacular, that Penelope didn't know where to look first. Large vases of flowers were scattered around the room; a grand fountain graced the center; and tables were covered with nibbles and delectables that smelled heavenly.

A band began to play music that

made Penelope long to dance, but she remembered the Weeby Way of Sit and Stay and forced herself to remain by Lady Diggleton's side. As Lady Diggleton spoke to her friends—many of whom had dogs of their own—Penelope did not bark or lunge. And when Lady Diggleton walked Penelope to the food-laden table, she did not beg. Instead, she waited patiently as Lady Diggleton selected tasty looking morsels for her.

But then Lady Diggleton did something Penelope did not expect: She led her onto the dance floor as the band began to play a waltz. Lady Diggleton did the steps, and Penelope soon got the idea, staying by her side perfectly, until they were dancing as though they'd been doing it all their lives!

Everyone, it seemed, stopped to look at them and Penelope, emboldened, did a little spin, which led to much clapping and laughter.

The waltz was just ending when Mr. Weeby was suddenly upon them. "My lady!" he said. "I have incredible news!"

"You often do, Mr. Weeby," said Lady Diggleton.

"The pug's dancing has caught the eye of the Queen, who requests an audience!"

"The Queen?" Lady Diggleton asked, amazed.

"The very same. She's waiting for you both!"

Can it be? Penelope thought nervously. *I am to meet the Queen? This is my chance to impress Lady Diggleton once and for all—or I could ruin everything.*

Penelope tried to calm herself as Lady Diggleton led her to a red carpet that stretched along a gallery. The Queen, as everyone knew, was fond of dogs, especially her own, a King Charles spaniel named Duchess. Both the Queen and her dog cast their regal gazes upon Penelope and Lady Diggleton as they approached, and they were most intimidating. "Steady yourself, Penelope," Lady Diggleton whispered to the little pug. "Although I must admit, my heart is racing so."

A footman announced them at top volume. "May I present Lady Diggleton and Penelope the pug!"

The time for Penelope to impress the Queen had arrived when she heard a familiar sound.

It was a chuckling, almost. More like a chittering, perhaps? It was, Penelope realized in horror, a sound she knew *very* well—the sound of Dreadful Squirrel!

From the corner of her eye, Penelope caught sight of him sitting in a window, munching on a tart he'd obviously stolen off one of the many, many carts. Penelope felt her temper begin to rise, and her heart began to race. Oh, but she wanted to chase that squirrel! She could just feel her legs, twitching and about ready to spring . . .

But suddenly she did something she never thought possible: She took a deep breath and ignored Dreadful Squirrel completely! Instead, she held her head up high and sat before the Queen.

"Oh my, what a charming pug," the Queen said, leaning down and offering her hand.

In return, Penelope offered a single paw to shake, and the entire gallery erupted in joyous applause.

The Queen shook Penelope's paw, then turned to Lady Diggleton. "I

commend you, Lady Diggleton, on your pug, and I proclaim her the top dog of this season's Begood Ball!"

The rest of the evening passed in a blur. Gentlemen and ladies lined up to meet Penelope, who was placed upon a chair so she could offer a paw to each in turn. Mr. Weeby stood by her side, of course, handing out his calling card and talking about the Weeby Way to anyone who would listen. Lady Diggleton, meanwhile, was smiling so hard her face began to hurt. She had not had so much fun in ever so long.

And so it was that a decision was made with Lady Diggleton's healing heart. Penelope would stay with her for good, for she knew with complete certainty that she and the little pug belonged to one another.

"I must tell you, Penelope," Lady Diggleton said to the pug's upturned face, "that you have made my life full again . . ."

Oh, this is it! Penelope thought, about to burst with joy.

"I would be most honored if you would stay with me for—"

"Lady Diggleton!"

Both dog and Lady turned, and there she was: Lady Picklebottom.

"I have just been met by a friend who says she knows Penelope's rightful owner!" she exclaimed.

"I beg your pardon?" Lady Diggleton said, sure she must have heard wrong. "What did you say?"

"I don't blame you for needing me to say it twice, for this is the news you have been awaiting for ever so long. Lady Foxwise has just informed me that she knows Penelope's former Lady!"

"But that can't be so," Lady Diggleton said.

"I assure you it is!" Lady Picklebottom

said. "Lady Foxwise has just left the ball, for she is older and her knees ached so, but we are invited to her home tomorrow, and there the mystery of whom Penelope belongs to will be solved once and for all!"

—

CHAPTER FOURTEEN

The following morning, Lady Diggleton was heartbroken. *Losing this pug will bring me such sorrow,* she thought as she pushed away her morning tea, *but the pug belongs to another. So I must show courage. I cannot be faint of heart.*

Penelope, meanwhile, was much the same. *I shall be devastated to lose Lady Diggleton,* she thought. *And I must admit, now that so much time has passed, I remember very little of my former Lady. Yet I must be brave . . .*

Thus, Penelope and Lady Diggleton rode in silence to Lady Foxwise's house, each looking forlornly out the carriage window. They did not want the ride to end, for that meant they would be deprived of the other's company. Yet the carriage came to a jolting halt before Lady Foxwise's door. The time to say goodbye was near, and both were in anguish because of it.

"Welcome, Lady Diggleton!" said Lady Picklebottom, who was standing on the front steps and grinning ear to ear. "Isn't this the most exciting day? Soon you shall be relieved of this responsibility, although may I say you have borne it

well, and Penelope will be returned to the Lady she must surely miss."

Neither dog nor lady could reply as they were shown into Lady Foxwise's sitting room. It is said that hers is one of the finest in London, but neither Penelope nor Lady Diggleton noticed a thing about it.

"I see our party has gathered!" boomed Lady Foxwise as she strode into the room, her neck strung with heavy pearls. "And to solve a mystery, no less. Could anything be more delightful? I certainly think not! But why so glum, my dear?" she asked, turning to Lady Diggleton. "Perhaps the excitement has exhausted you. But do not fret, for I am about to reveal all."

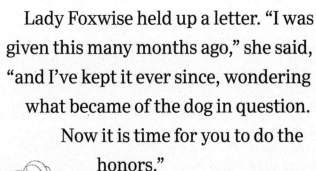

Lady Foxwise held up a letter. "I was given this many months ago," she said, "and I've kept it ever since, wondering what became of the dog in question. Now it is time for you to do the honors."

Penelope watched as Lady Foxwise handed Lady Diggleton the letter.

I must accept whatever comes, Penelope reminded herself, *for although I am just a little pug, I can still be as brave as the largest of hounds.*

Fearing she would cry, Lady Diggleton did not delay. She opened the letter, and began to read aloud . . .

To whoever has found my dearest pug, I am writing this letter in the hopes that someone has found my darling Penelope. I lost her in Puggleton Park when she raced off to catch the most dreadful squirrel I have ever had the displeasure to meet. Since then, I have searched high and low, and I have called her name many times, even in my dreams. Yet I could not find her. Now I must leave London, for I am going to live in the country with my sister, who has suddenly found herself in need of my assistance.

It is with great sadness that I must report that my lovely sister is allergic to dogs, and I shall not be able to have Penelope with me at her farm even if she is found. Therefore, it is my dearest wish that, if you have found my pug, you will decide to keep her. Penelope is the most wonderful dog I have ever known, you see, and I promise that her presence will bring you nothing but the greatest joy in all the world.

Most sincerely,
Lady Applestone

"What?" said Lady Picklebottom, reaching for the letter. "There must be some mistake!" She turned to Lady Diggleton. "Surely Lady Applestone's mind could be changed," she said. "I shall seek her sister's farm out at once and remind her how much she loves her precious pug."

"But Lady Applestone is not asking for Penelope to be returned," said Lady Foxwise, "because her sister's health will not allow it."

"Someone else, then," said Lady Picklebottom. "Surely a different farm will take her . . ."

Lady Foxwise laughed. "My dear Lady Picklebottom! I'm afraid you are very much off the mark! Can't you see that Lady Diggleton and the pug are overjoyed by this news? To try to keep them apart would hurt the friend you claim to care so much about."

At this, Lady Picklebottom looked at Lady Diggleton, who was crying with joy, and at Penelope, whose tail was wagging as fast as it could. At the sight, Lady Picklebottom found herself unable to speak, perhaps for the first time in her life.

"Come to me, my darling!" Lady Diggleton said, getting down upon the floor.

So Penelope, forgetting all about the Weeby Way of Sit and Stay, ran to her new Lady, leaped into her lap, and covered her face with kisses.

"I don't understand," said Lady Picklebottom, "why you are so happy."

Turning to see Lady Picklebottom's confusion, Lady Diggleton took pity on

her. "Thank you, my friend, for your kind assistance in solving the mystery of Penelope's original owner," she said. "You have done me a wonderful kindness. For now that I know about Lady Applestone and her sister, I can rest easy that Penelope and I will stay together for good." She paused, looking down at her pug. "May I also announce to you, Penelope, that I shall never again insist that you do the Weeby Way of Sit and Stay. Nor shall I keep you off my lap at tea, or dinner, or any other place. We shall snuggle, dance, and frolic all we want, and there is nothing anyone in London can say or do about it!"

"But—" said Lady Picklebottom.

"A happy ending has been found,"

said Lady Foxwise. "And I do believe we have heard quite enough from you, Lady Picklebottom. So let's have tea, my dear."

After a most lovely tea, during which Penelope remained on Lady Diggleton's lap, they said their farewells. Outside, Lady Diggleton put Penelope on her leash and said, "Thank you, Lady Foxwise, for giving me the letter. I do hope you will let us visit you again soon."

"I will insist upon it!" said Lady Foxwise.

"Then it is time to bring my sweet pug to our forever home," said Lady Diggleton, "for I am her forever Lady."

As they ran up the street, passersby

turned to stare. But Penelope and Lady Diggleton did not care a bit. Happiness was what they were after now—and the chance to always be themselves.

As they neared Lady Diggleton's house, they heard someone calling behind them, "Stop! You must stop!"

They turned to see who it was. It was Lady Picklebottom!

"Wait!" she called. "Please wait for me!"

Penelope and Lady Diggleton

were both surprised to see her running so. In fact, Lady Diggleton could not think of a time that Lady Picklebottom had ever moved so fast.

Lady Picklebottom caught up to them and tried to catch her breath. "It is true that I have always believed that animals belong on a farm," she said, panting hard. "And, as you know, I am not often wrong. But perhaps I was on this *one* occasion. Which is why I have bought Penelope the perfect gift."

What on earth could it be? wondered Penelope, for she simply could not believe that Lady Picklebottom would get her something she would desire.

Lady Picklebottom handed Lady Diggleton a bag from the pet emporium, and Penelope watched as

her Lady opened the bag, then laughed.
"I do believe you are right this time,
my friend," she said, "that this is the
perfect gift. But now we must see if
Penelope agrees."

Nodding, Lady Picklebottom leaned
down and gently placed a toy at
Penelope's feet.

To the pug's great surprise, it was the
best gift she could possibly imagine!
It was not a ball, or a stick. It was her
very own toy squirrel, you see, with
a raggedy tail, and the most terrible
buckteeth she had ever seen.

And it was absolutely, wonderfully
dreadful.